Chesapeake Bay Middle

Media

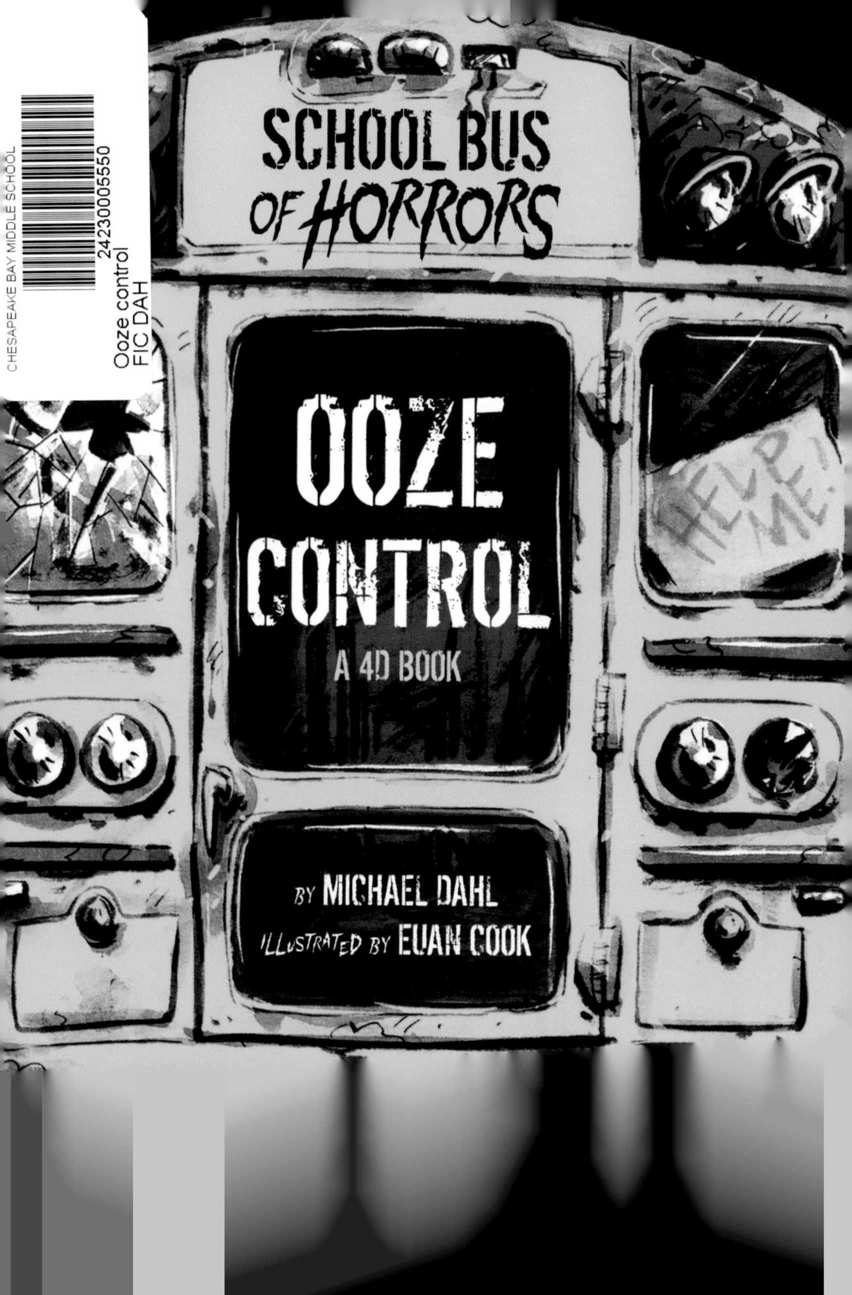
SCHOOL BUS OF HORRORS
OOZE CONTROL
A 4D BOOK
HELP ME!
BY MICHAEL DAHL
ILLUSTRATED BY EUAN COOK

School Bus of Horrors is published by
Stone Arch Books
A Capstone Imprint
1710 Roe Crest Drive
North Mankato, Minnesota 56003
www.mycapstone.com

Cataloging-in-Publication Data is available at the Library of Congress website.
ISBN 978-1-4965-7835-8 (library binding)
ISBN 978-1-4965-8019-1 (paperback)
ISBN 978-1-4965-7840-2 (eBook PDF)

Summary: After school, a boy boards an odd-looking bus. Inside, the floor, the seats, and even the ceiling are covered with chewed-up wads of gum. Soon, the sticky wads grow thicker, climb higher, and come alive! Can the boy escape before the ooze takes control?

Designer: Sarah Bennett
Production Specialist: Tori Abraham

Cover background by Shutterstock/oldmonk

Printed in the United States of America.
PA49

1 Ask an adult to download the app.  Capstone 4D
Education

2 Scan any page with the star.

3 Enjoy your cool stuff!

———— OR ————

Use this password at capstone4D.com

ooze.78358

TABLE OF CONTENTS

From dawn to dusk, the **SCHOOL BUS OF HORRORS** rumbles along city streets and down country roads, searching for another passenger. Yellow, black markings, dirty windows—it looks like any other.

But **BEWARE!** Step aboard this bus and
experience the scariest ride of your life . . .

CHAPTER ONE
GROSS

Franco is starving when he gets on the bus after school.

"Why didn't you eat at lunch?" asks his friend Bella.

Franco rolls his eyes. "Because of the silly Carnival Days lunch menu," he says.

Bella nods. "But the food was so much fun!"

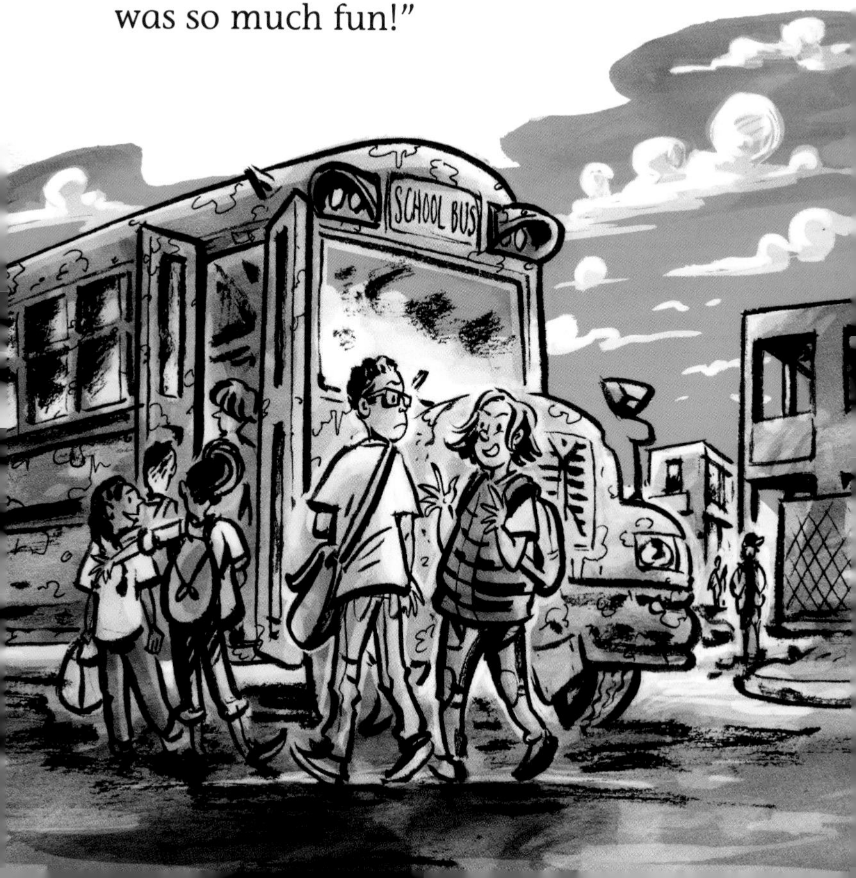
SCHOOL BUS

"Circus food," Franco says.
He groans.

"Cotton candy," adds Bella.
"And ice cream and candied apples."

"Exactly," says Franco with a
shiver. "Didn't you see how messy
that food is?"

"So what?" asks Bella.

"Sticky, gooey, drippy food," says
Franco. "Gross! I'd rather die."

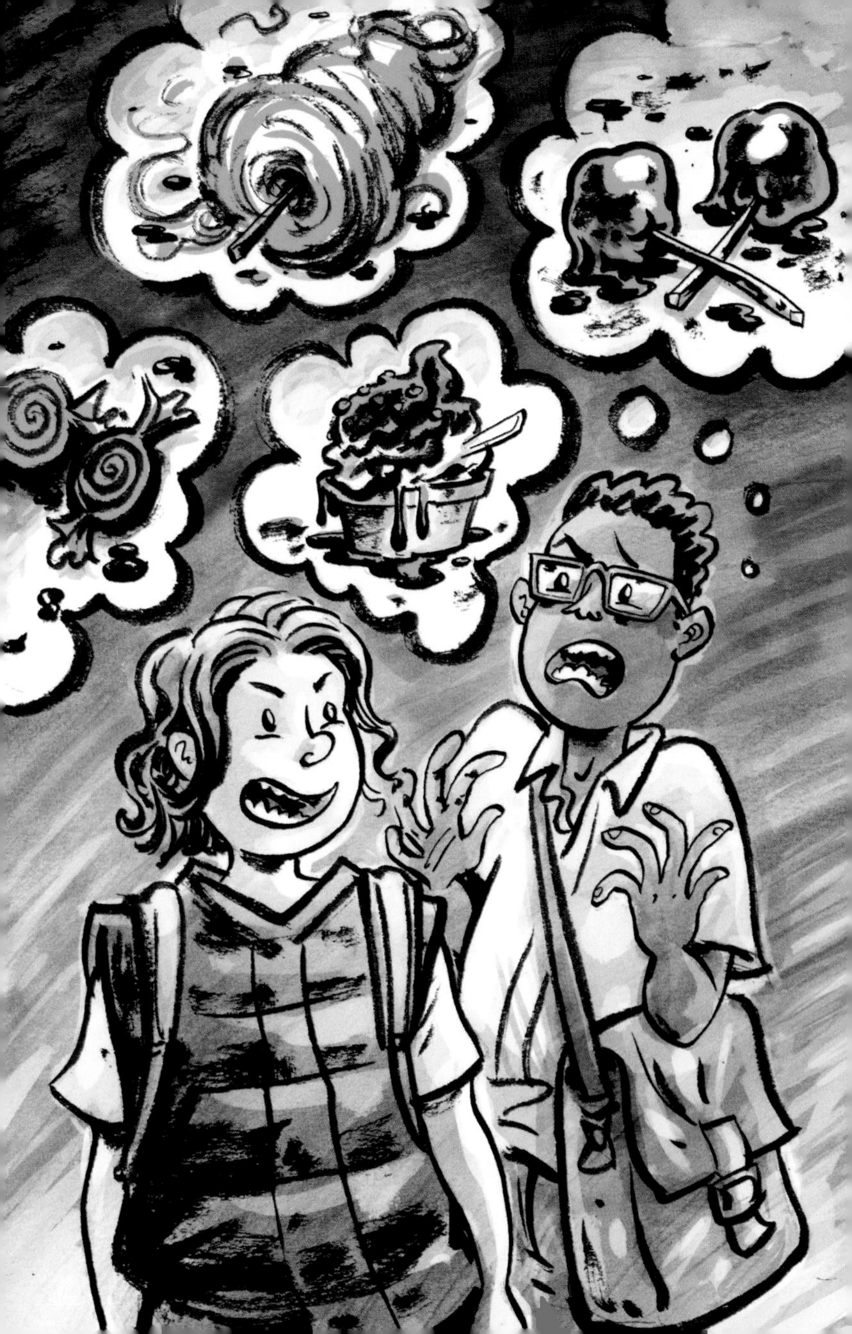

Franco brushes dirt off the bus seat before sitting down.

After he sits, he suddenly lifts his foot.

"Speaking of gross," he says.

Bella looks down at his shoe. "Gum?" she asks.

"The floor didn't have gum on it this morning," Franco says.

Franco looks around.

"And this isn't the same bus from this morning," he adds.

Bella looks toward the driver. "I've never seen him before, either," she says.

"And why does he sit inside that plastic box?" Franco asks.

"Probably a safety thing," says Bella.

"Looks like a smart idea to me," says Franco. "He doesn't have to touch all this grossness!"

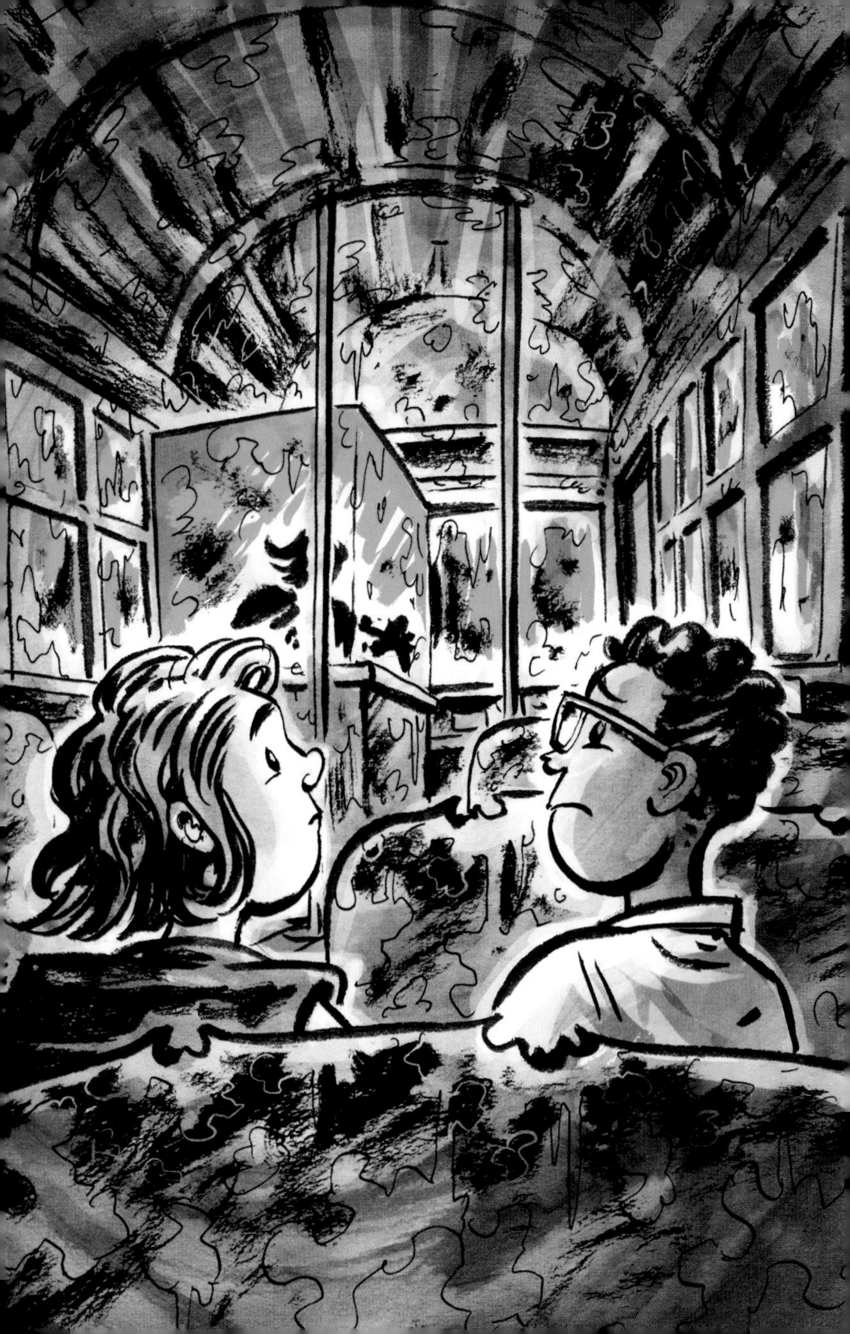

CHAPTER TWO
GUMMY

Just then, the strange bus hits a bump in the road.

The other passengers laugh, but Franco cries out.

"Ow!" he yells. "I bumped my knee against the seat."

Franco looks closely at the metal back of the seat ahead of him. The surface is covered with gum, old candy, and dead flies.

He doesn't even want to think about the other mysterious goop on there.

Franco carefully checks his knee.

"At least you didn't get anything on your pants," Bella says.

Franco smiles.

Then his face changes. "Are you chewing gum?" he asks angrily.

Bella doesn't look at him. "So what if I am?" she says.

Franco shakes his head. "It's people like you who make this gunky mess," he says.

Bella stares hard at him. "Well, don't worry," she says. "I'm not going to spit out my—"

WHUMP! The strange bus hits another bump.

Bella is surprised and coughs.

"Patooey!" She accidentally spits out her gum.

Bella's gum flies past Franco's ear. The chewed-up wad sticks to the window next to his head.

"Sorry about that," says Bella, feeling her cheeks burn. "Please, could you hand it back?"

Franco's eyes widen.

"You think I'm going to touch that?" he cries. "That gum was in your mouth!"

CHAPTER THREE
GOOEY

Franco stands up.

"Switch places with me," he tells Bella. "I'm not sitting next to your spit."

"It's just gum!" says Bella.
She is angry.

"Gross," says Franco. He grabs the metal pole next to their seat.

The metal pole is covered with something green and sticky.

"Hey, I'm stuck," says Franco. "I can't move my hand."

"Hehehehehehee!"

Franco turns his head and looks at the bus driver.

"Were you just laughing at me?" he asks the driver.

He doesn't get an answer. But through the plastic box, Franco spots a wicked smile.

CHAPTER FOUR
STICKY

WHUMP! The bus bumps again.

Franco's hand is free of the pole,
but the bump knocks him backward.

SQQQUIIRRSHHH!

He falls in the middle of the dirty aisle between the rows of seats.

The aisle is slick like snot.

"Yuck!" Franco shouts.

He feels sticky and oozy gunk on the back of his head and neck.

Then he feels something else.
The gunk is crawling on him!

"Help me!" Franco cries.
He reaches up to the seat.

Franco can't see Bella from the floor. But he can see more ooze sliding down the metal poles.

The aisle fills with slime. The slime is covered with the crud that was stuck to the bus's floor.

Crumbs from chocolate crispy bars.

Syrupy waffles.

The rotting skins of peaches and oranges.

The goopy crusts from peanut butter sandwiches.

Gum.

Lots of gum!

CHAPTER FIVE
OOZING CONTROL

Franco can't lift himself up toward the seats.

Everything he tries to grab is covered with the slick stuff.

The aisle beneath him starts to change. It sinks and rises like a bouncy mattress.

The seats are melting.

All the students slide into the aisle of slime around Franco.

Franco sees Bella's arm as she sinks beneath the slime.

"Driver!" shouts Franco.

The driver is no longer there.

The windshield is also gone. In its place, Franco sees a deep, dark pit.

The aisle of ooze slopes down toward the pit. Franco slides down the slippery aisle faster and faster.

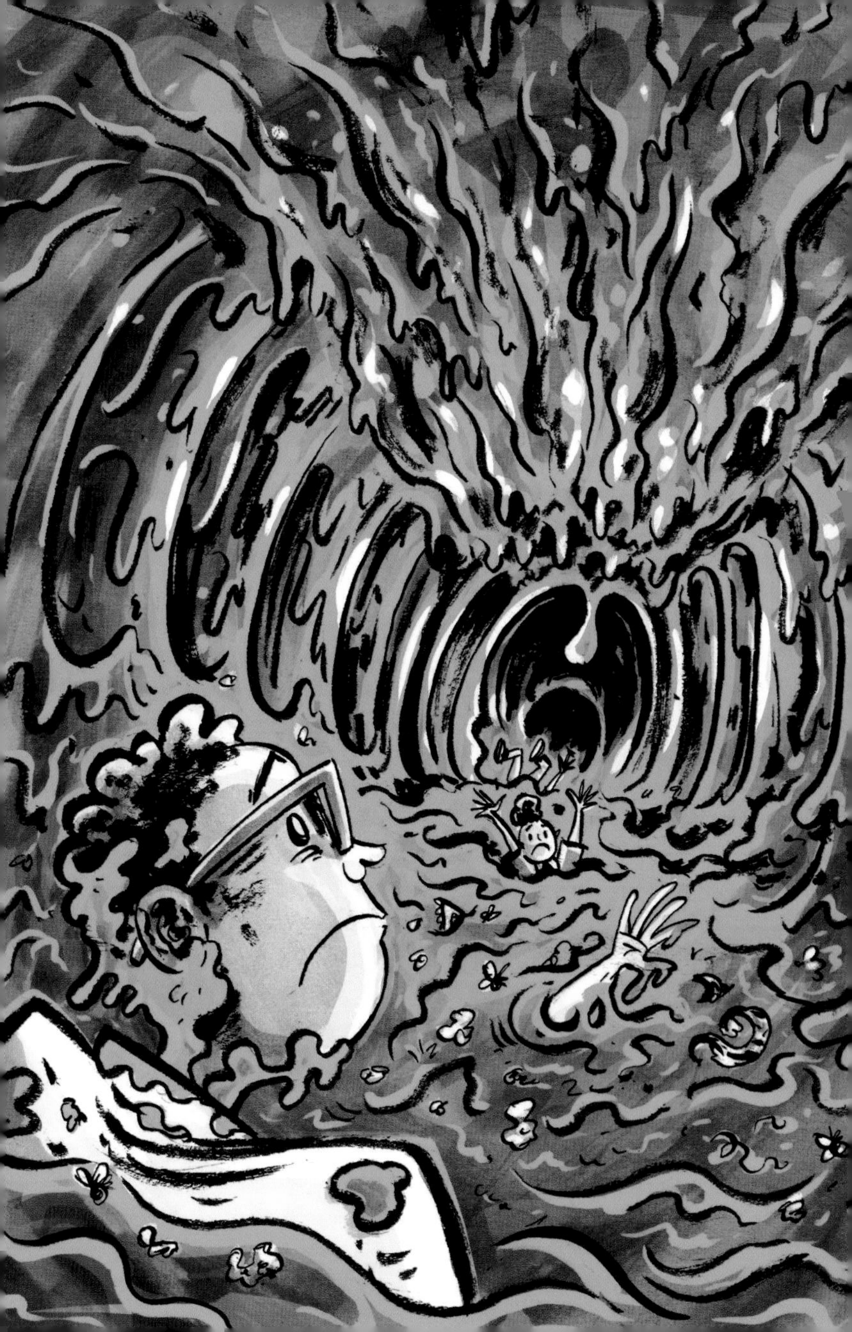

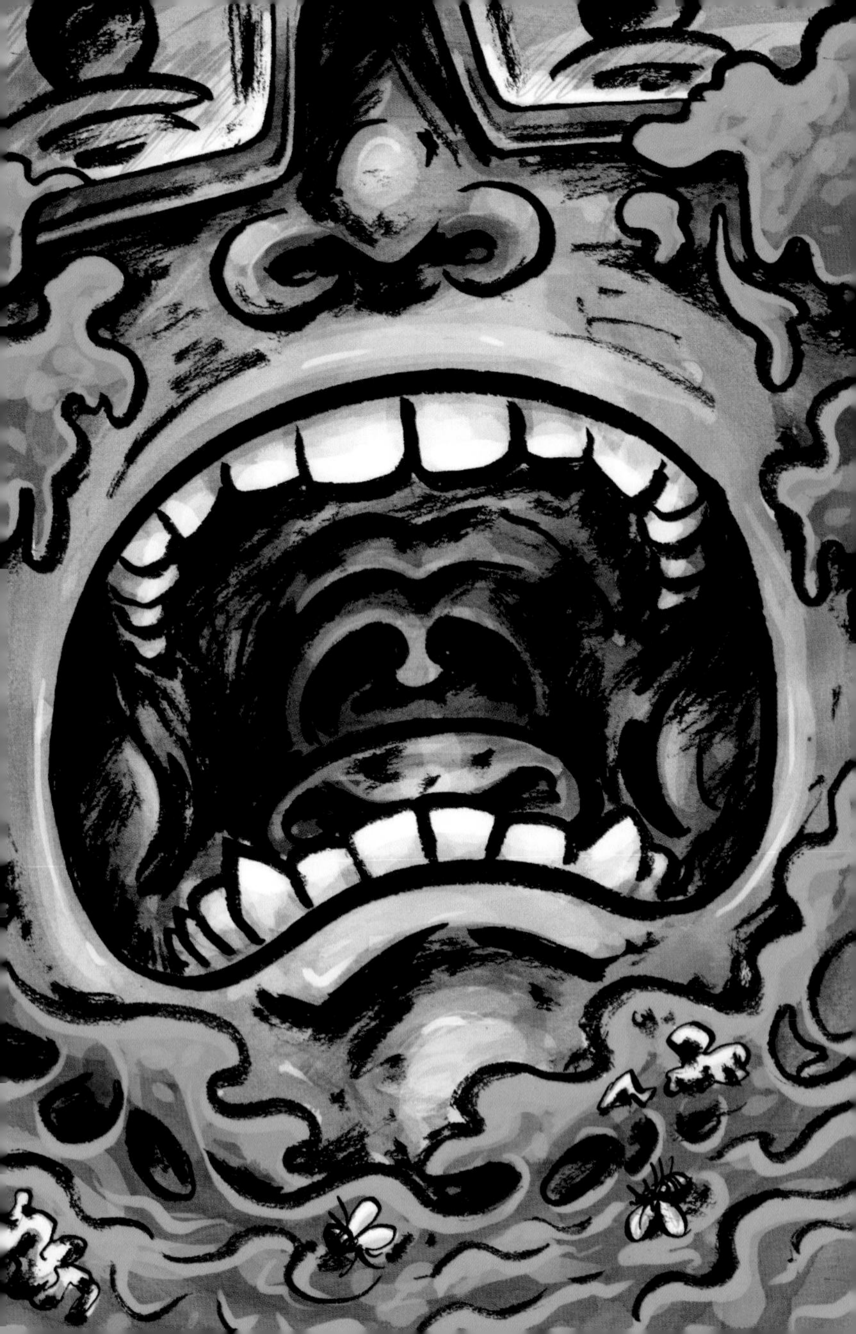

"NoOOoooOoo!" Franco screams.

When Franco first stepped on the bus, he was starving.

He didn't realize that the bus was too!

GLOSSARY

AISLE (ILE)—a path that runs between rows of seats

CARNIVAL (KAR-nuh-vuhl)—a public celebration, often with rides and games

GOOEY (GOO-ee)—sticky

GUNK (GUNGK)—something that is filthy, sticky, or greasy

MYSTERIOUS (miss-TIHR-ee-uhss)—hard to explain or understand

SALIVA (suh-LYE-vuh)—the clear liquid in your mouth that helps you swallow and begin to digest food

SURFACE (SUR-fiss)—the ouside layer of something

DISCUSS

1. Why do you think the author titled this book *Ooze Control*?

2. What are some of your least favorite foods? Why do you dislike them so much?

3. What is your favorite illustration in this book? Describe why it's your favorite.

WRITE

1. Create a new title for this book. Then write a paragraph on why you chose your new title.

2. Do you think the bus will swallow Franco or spit him out? Write another chapter to this story to describe what happens next.

3. Write about the scariest bus ride you've ever experienced.

AUTHOR

MICHAEL DAHL is the author of the best-selling Library of Doom series, the Dragonblood books, and Michael Dahl's Really Scary Stories. (He wants everyone to know that last title was not his idea.) He was born a few minutes after midnight of April Fool's Day in a thunderstorm, has survived various tornados and hurricanes, as well as an attack from a rampant bunny at night ("It reared up at me!"). He currently lives in a haunted house and once saw a ghost in his high school. He will never ride on a school bus. These stories will explain why.

ILLUSTRATOR

EUAN COOK is an illustrator from London, who enjoys drawing pictures for books and watching foxes and jays out his window. He also likes walking around looking at broken brickwork, sooty statues, and the weird drainpipes and stuff you can find behind old run-down buildings.

SCHOOL BUS OF HORRORS

AUTO BODY PARTS

NIGHT SHIFT

OOZE CONTROL

SHOCKS!

CRUSH HOUR

DEAD END

DESTRUCTION ZONE

FRIDAY NIGHT HEADLIGHTS

THE SQUEALS ON THE BUS

UNDER THE HOOD